PATIENCE BREWSTER

Little, Brown and Company

Boston Toronto London

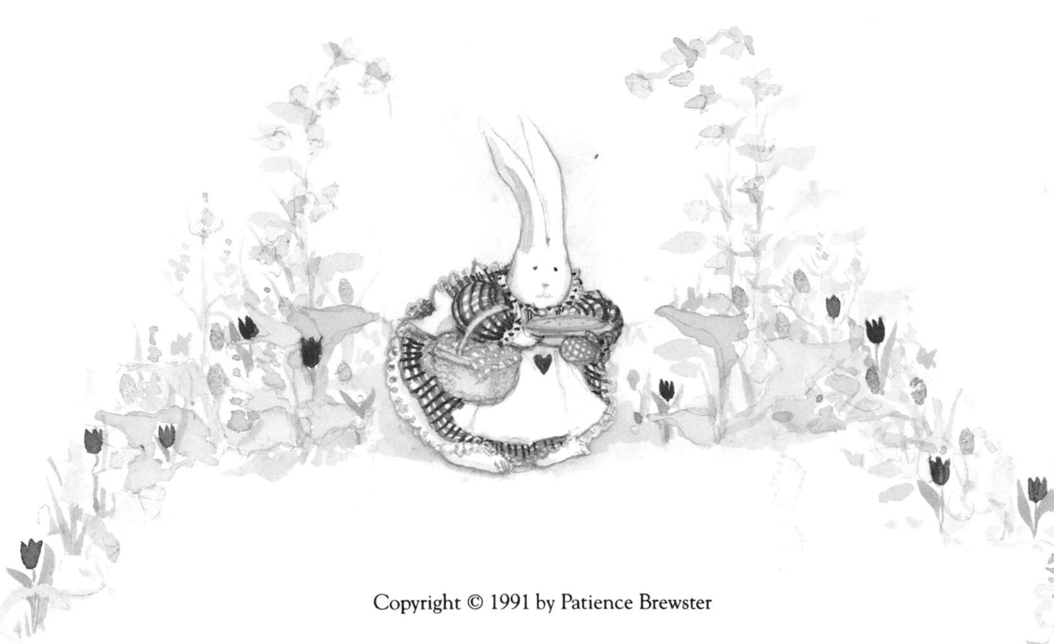

First edition

Library of Congress Cataloging-in-Publication Data

Brewster, Patience.
Rabbit Inn/written and illustrated by Patience Brewster. — 1st ed.
p. cm.
Summary: The impending arrival of very special guests at Rabbit Inn causes Pandora and her husband to assign their other animal guests a multitude of tasks for getting the inn ready.
ISBN 0-316-10747-6
[1. Hotels, motels, etc. — Fiction. 2. Rabbits — Fiction. 3. Animals — Fiction. 4. Babies — Fiction.] I. Title.
PZ7.B7572Rab 1991
[E] — dc20 89-13668

10 9 8 7 6 5 4 3 2 1

WOR

Published simultaneously in Canada
by Little, Brown & Company (Canada) Limited

Printed in the United States of America

LUPINE
FOR ROGER HANDAL STILL MY GOOD FRIEND, MY INSPIRATION, AND MY FAVORITE PAINTER
FOR HOLLY, FOR BEING BOB AND GETTING ME MY JOB
FOR MY WONDERFUL SISTER AND BELOVED FRIEND, MARLEE
VIOLET
THANK · YOU MARIA & DILYS THE HONORED RABBIT GOD MOTHERS
FLOWERS

This is the Rabbit Inn.

These are the rabbits who live in the inn, Pandora and Bob Lapinandro. Mr. Lapinandro grows flowers and fruit and delectable vegetables for Mrs. Lapinandro's fabulous feasts. Up to now they have been very happy here tending to their gardens and guests, and no one minded the viney twiney yard, or the dusty musty corners of the old and homey inn.

Until one day Pandora Lapinandro was leaning against her rickety picket fence when news arrived that some very special visitors were on their way to the Rabbit Inn. She looked around at her tumbledown home and thought, "Oh, no! Oh, no, no, no! This won't do! No, this won't do at all!" She was shocked by all that needed to be done and done right away.

First she whispered her secret to Bob.

Then she started a list of jobs.

The list began with raking and staking, and stacking and packing, fixing the leaks and oiling the squeaks. Next she listed items to clean, to paint or to polish to a sparkling sheen.

Bob took one look at the list as it grew and said, "There's much too much to do! There aren't enough nails, there aren't enough pails, there's not enough time for a list this long!"

"Hogwash!" said Pandora and added to the list:

BUY MORE NAILS
GET MORE PAILS

So this is how it went: the rabbits scraped and raked. They scrubbed and rubbed. They took down curtains, they shook out rugs. Bob kept hoping Pandora would be satisfied.

"I think it looks a lot better! Don't you?"

But every time Pandora looked up, she added something new:

SEW TORN CURTAINS
MEND WORN RUGS

Soon Bob made no more comments. He just worked fast and furiously trying to shorten the list.

But the list continued to grow.

Bob needed help. He knocked on the door of room number 1. That was the door of the Gluckadores. When the chickens heard of his predicament, they were happy to help.

"Heaven's sakes, Bob, give us a job!" The plucky chickens checked the list and bustled about without delay, Henry picking up here and Clucky pecking away.

Bob felt so much better.

But he didn't feel better for long! Even with the chickens' help, Pandora's list lengthened. So Bob climbed up to see Penny and Quickie in room number 3. The squirrels glanced at his list and gasped at its length. They briskly adjusted their tails for the task of whisking about at some buffing and puffing. To polish and shine was a snap for the squirrels, but when Bob was gone, they nervously whispered, "Who do you think this guest could be? That's the question we just can't ignore. . . . Whom are we dusting the must away for?"

RABBIT INN

The next morning Bob was up early, reluctantly knocking at the Rumpletons' door. He did not expect the pigs to help, but the list included "garbage removal," which got Ralph and Tiny's instant approval. Each offered pointy feet and snout for garden tilling and weeding out.

So it was official. There were two more helpers.

Mrs. Lapinandro was thrilled with her guests. She thanked them and thanked them, but she still couldn't rest. She just kept finding more things to be done. Now the long list was tacked up like a banner. All the guests wondered, because of her manner, *"Who is coming? Who could it be? A duke, a duchess, Rabbit Royalty?"*

BROCCOLI
CAULIFLOWER
CARROTS
BEETS
RADISH
MARIGOLDS
DILL WEED
BASIL
PARSLEY
JERUSALEM
ARTICHOKE
CHECK
ASPARAGUS
BULBS
PETUNIAS
PANSIES
PEONIES
IMPATIENCE
LOBELIA
SNAPDRAGONS
VIOLAS
KITCHEN
SHELVES
FIX THE SQUEAK
ON THE PANTRY
STOP THE
DROP IN THE
KITCHEN FAUCET
WASHERS
NEED TO BE
REPLACED
PAINT
WHITEWASH
SWEEP THE
DRIVEWAY
HOSE IT
DOWN
TAKE DOWN
SHUTTERS
PAINT A
LAVENDER
MULCH AND
CUT BACK THE

Up in the attic while storing some boxes, Bob woke up the inn's tiniest guests. The Eeks had heard about all the commotion, and the little mice wished they could assist. Poor tired Bob couldn't think of a way, but instead of refusing, he consulted the list. Weezie Eek squeaked and dashed for her basket. She had spotted a task before Bob could ask. She and Beenie streaked downstairs. In less than a minute they were sewing and stitching and making repairs.

The only guests not yet in the frenzy were Olive Longbottom and Gertie Snew, the elderly cats in room number 2. They were musical cats with backgrounds in opera and they also excelled at the telling of tales. Bob said, “Yes! We all could use some diversion.” The cats were ecstatic! They tuned up their voices and pruned back their whiskers. They snatched up their purses, their powder, and hankies and padded downstairs all set to perform.

The cats did the trick! Their singing and spinning of rip-roaring yarns made the polishing and mending, the spicking and spanning, the speedy ship-shaping go zipping right by.

That night, when the animals were heading for bed, they all were wondering, "*Who are we expecting?*" Quietly smiling, Pandora admitted she wasn't quite certain, but please understand, they all had to trust her; the guests would be grand. And no one should doubt what this fuss was about. So long into evening, Pandora kept cleaning, the rest of them dreaming she'd run out of jobs. Especially Bob.

WASH RAGS
AND LAUNDRY BAGS
CHANGE SHEETS
PICKLE BEETS
BUY SOAP
BUY ROPE
SCRUB TUB
~~PRUNE TREES~~
~~DIG WEEDS~~
~~BURN LEAVES~~
~~STORE SEEDS~~

Now without anyone knowing . . . the list stopped growing! Things were rapidly being crossed off. Pandora was snowed with the glowing results, and she finally seemed to be slowing down.

All that was left was one daily chore for each animal guest. Hooray! Hurrah! This was quite an occasion! The table was set with everyone's treats! Sweets, cherry pies, carrot cakes, and oat muffins . . . The animals sat back to admire the inn!

Now that the place was so inviting, *just who were the guests* they'd soon be delighting? But weary Pandora would merely say, "It won't be long now. They're well on their way!"

For the first time in four weeks, there was time to relax. No laundry to press, just checkers and chess. No mops or sponges, nothing to shine. Pandora said, "Thank you," at least forty-nine times.

Especially to Bob.

At first morning light, Bob was out in the garden. But not to weed, not intending to prune. Today he picked flowers and whistled a tune! He picked nine dahlias, ten pansies and lilies, and twelve pretty roses to bring to his wife . . . and to the punctual guests who arrived last night.

"My land!" said Pandora. "We were ready in time! The inn looks divine for these fine guests of mine!"

NICHOLAS
LILLY
CHARLOTTE
LEONIDE
LIZZY
EZR
CUPCAKE
CHARLES
RACHAEL
OTTO
HIGGINS
ROSE
JOSEPHINE
MARTHA
MILLY
TILLY RASTUS
TATIANNA WILLY
DILYS
SARAH
ELLIS
EMILY
JILLY
TAMES
ROGER
PEARL
JELLY BEAN
LYDIA
LOIS
HEATHER
HANNAH
LUCY
OPAL
JOHNNO
HATTIE
KATE
ELIZABETH
HERM
SPENCER
MARIETTA
ISABELLE
ELLIOT
HOLLY
SAM BEN
LOUISE
RASPBERRY
WENDY
MARIA
IRA-ANNE
POPPY
ELLEN
CYNTHIA
IRIS

And that was just ducky for Henry and Clucky, for Weezie and Beenie and Tiny, too! And what about Ralph and Penny and Quickie? They were nearly as delighted as Olive and Gertie. They were just as proud of the inn and its mob as the new parents — Pandora and Bob.